The Poombah of Badoombah

To poombah means to impart, or infuse with, extraordinary energy.
A Poombah is one renowned for having this power.
The word is my own invention, *Badoombah beans* my oldest son's.

The Poombah of Badoombah

BY **DEE LILLEGARD**

ILLUSTRATED BY
KEVIN HAWKES

G.P. PUTNAM'S SONS

What does it mean?

Bombay — a large city in India

mridanga — an Indian drum that is barrel-shaped and made of clay or a hollowed-out block of wood

rajah — a prince or chief in India.

dervish — a religious beggar. Dervishes are also known for their whirling dances.

howdah — a canopied seat on the back of a camel or elephant

nabob — a governor of a town or district in India, or a very rich man

he Poombah of Badoombah
was mightier than any king,
for *he* had the power
to poombah *anything*.

He poombahed the potter
at his wheel one day,
and pots,
    POTS,
        POTS
leaped out of the clay.

He poombahed the weaver
working at his loom,
and carpets flew magically,
filling his room.

The Poombah sent a pudgy rajah
swirling to the public bath.

The Poombah sent a nervous dervish
whirling down a curvish path.

He sent a drummer's mridanga *booming!*
He sent a merchant's spices *zooming*—
ginger, pepper, cinnamon, cloves—
into the monkeys' mango groves.

But at the swarming street bazaar,
the Poombah of Badoombah went too far. . . .

A nabob bound for old Bombay
came riding in a howdah.
He sat upon an elephant
so very high and proud,
a jewel in his turban.
All his servants humbly bowed.

And *then* . . .

The Poombah of Badoombah
sent the elephant a *zing!*
The nabob, that poor fellow, went
*boing-boing*ing like a spring.

The whole bazaar was scattered . . . zomped . . .
as elephant and rider romped.

When things were quiet, less disjointed,
fingers, angry fingers, pointed. . . .

"The Poombah of Badoombah did it.
Show the man no pity!"
Their power all together
made the Poombah flee the city.

Now somewhere in the countryside,
removed from urban scenes,
the Poombah of Badoombah grows . . .
what else—*Badoombah beans!*

Peacefully the Poombah lolls
within a shady bower,
glad to let his beans contain
his lavish magic power.

They hop. They jump. They all but shout.
Let no one disbelieve or doubt . . .
a bowl of Badoombah beans or two
is all one needs for a hullaballoo.

To Brett — and his co-conspirators,
Collin, April, and Marcos — D.L.

To Ian — K.H.

Text copyright © 1998 by Dee Lillegard

Illustrations copyright © 1998 by Kevin Hawkes

All rights reserved. This book, or parts thereof, may not be reproduced in any form without permission in writing from the publisher. G. P. Putnam's Sons, a division of The Putnam & Grosset Group, 200 Madison Avenue, New York, NY 10016 G. P. Putnam's Sons, Reg. U.S. Pat. & Tm. Off. Published simultaneously in Canada Printed in Hong Kong by South China Printing Co. (1988) Ltd. Design by Gunta Alexander. Text set in Berkeley Old Style. Library of Congress Cataloging-in-Publication Data Lillegard, Dee. The Poombah of Badoombah / by Dee Lillegard; illustrated by Kevin Hawkes. p. cm. Summary: When the powerful but mischievous Poombah of Badoombah finally takes things a bit too far, he is forced to flee the city and live out the rest of his days in the quiet of the countryside. [1.India—Fiction. 2. Markets—Fiction. 3. Stories in rhyme. 4. Humorous stories.] I. Hawkes, Kevin, ill. II. Title. PZ8.3.L6144Po 1998 [E]—dc21 97-9615 CIP AC ISBN 0-399-22778-4 10 9 8 7 6 5 4 3 2 1 First Impression